Nerdy Birdy

TWEETS

STORY BY
Aaron Reynolds

PICTURES BY
Matt Davies

A NEAL PORTER BOOK
ROARING BROOK PRESS
NEW YORK

This is Nerdy Birdy.

Nerdy Birdy loves playing video games.

OFFICIA

HELLO B
LUNCH

This is Vulture.

Vulture thinks video
games are boring.
Vulture loves snacking on
dead things. Nerdy Birdy
thinks dead things are gross.

Nerdy Birdy and Vulture are very different.
They are also best friends.

Three things Nerdy Birdy and Vulture love to do together:

GLUTEN-, FLAVOR-, TEXTURE- & EXCITEMENT- FREE **Bread crumbs**

EDIBLE PRODUCT

1. Make fun of each other's lunch.

2. Make silly faces.

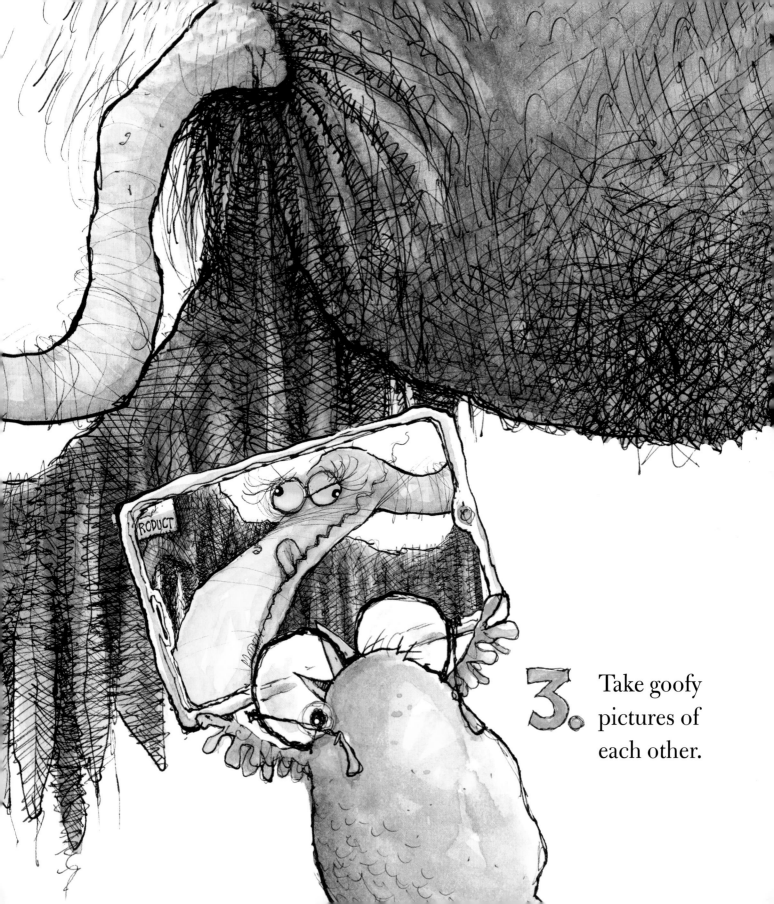

3. Take goofy pictures of each other.

One day, Nerdy Birdy discovered
an amazing new game.

"IT'S CALLED TWEETSTER,"
he told Vulture.

"WHAT DOES IT DO?"
asked Vulture.

"LOTS OF THINGS."

1. Collect tons of friends online who may, or may not, text you back.

2. Play games with them all.

3. Tweet messages and pictures for them all to see!

"SOUNDS, UM, AWESOME,"

said Vulture, even though it really sounded kind of dull.

An hour later, Nerdy Birdy had fifty new Tweetster friends.

"I'M FRIENDS WITH A FLAMINGO!"

"NEAT."

A day later, Nerdy Birdy had one hundred new Tweetster friends. He played Angry Worms with an ostrich and tweeted his score.

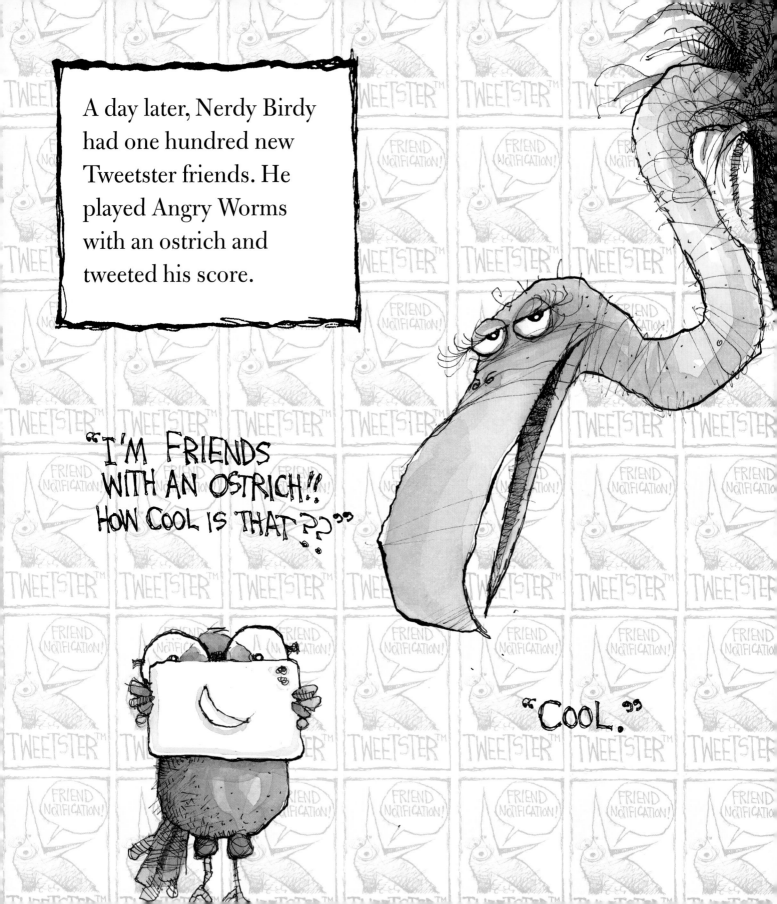

A week later, Nerdy Birdy had five hundred new Tweetster friends. He had never dreamed he could have that many friends.

"I'M FRIENDS WITH A PUFFIN!!

SHE LIVES IN ICELAND. ICELAND!!"

Vulture decided she'd had enough of
watching Nerdy Birdy play Tweetster.
Vulture spread her wings and flew away.

An hour later,
Nerdy Birdy
finally noticed.

The next day, Vulture
had a surprise for
Nerdy Birdy. Vulture
had joined Tweetster!

They Tweetstered—
TOGETHER!—all
morning.

At lunchtime, they put away their games. It was just like old times.

They made fun of each other's lunch.

They made silly faces. They took goofy pictures of each other.

But when they logged back on to Tweetster, Vulture found a surprise waiting for her.

"WHAT IS THIS!?"

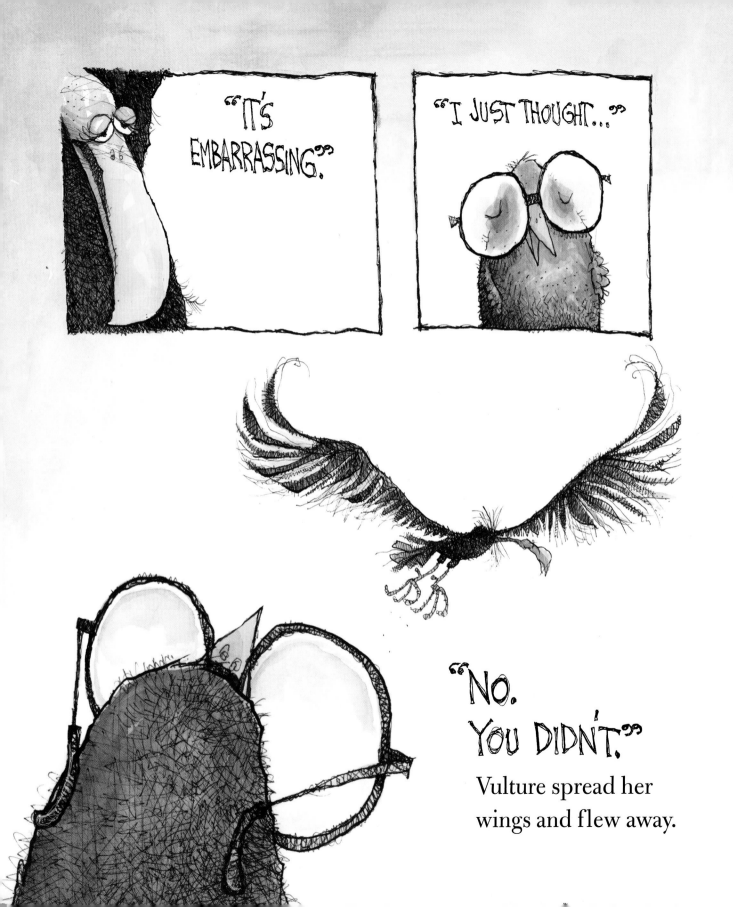

Vulture spread her
wings and flew away.

An hour later, Vulture hadn't come back to their favorite telephone wire.

A day later, Vulture still wouldn't answer any of Nerdy Birdy's calls.

VULTURE?!!

A week later, Nerdy Birdy found a
dead squirrel on the road. Vulture's
favorite snack. He waited for hours,
hoping she might stop by.

Vulture never
showed up.

But then it hit him.
Nerdy Birdy had five
hundred Tweetster
friends! He'd ask
them for advice.

He tweeted:

Ten minutes later, nobody had tweeted back.

An hour later, nobody had tweeted back.

A day later, only three Tweetster friends had tweeted back.

@PUFFINSTUFF

What do you want me to do about it? I LIVE IN ICELAND!!

Unhelpful.

@OSTRICH49

LOL!! STINKS 2 BU!!

Super unhelpful.

@PINKFLAMINGO7

Try not to be such a BIRD BRAIN. LOL!!

It wasn't meant to be helpful.

But it was. Super-duper helpful.

Nerdy Birdy closed down
his game. He opened up his
tiny little wings. And he flew.

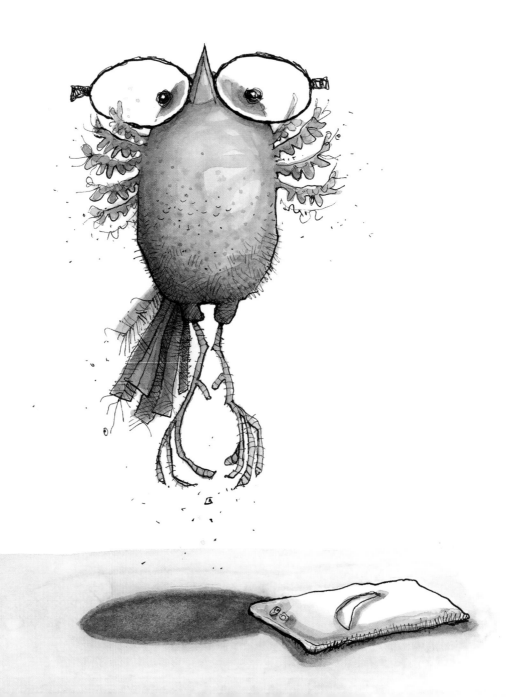

He flew high.

He flew low.

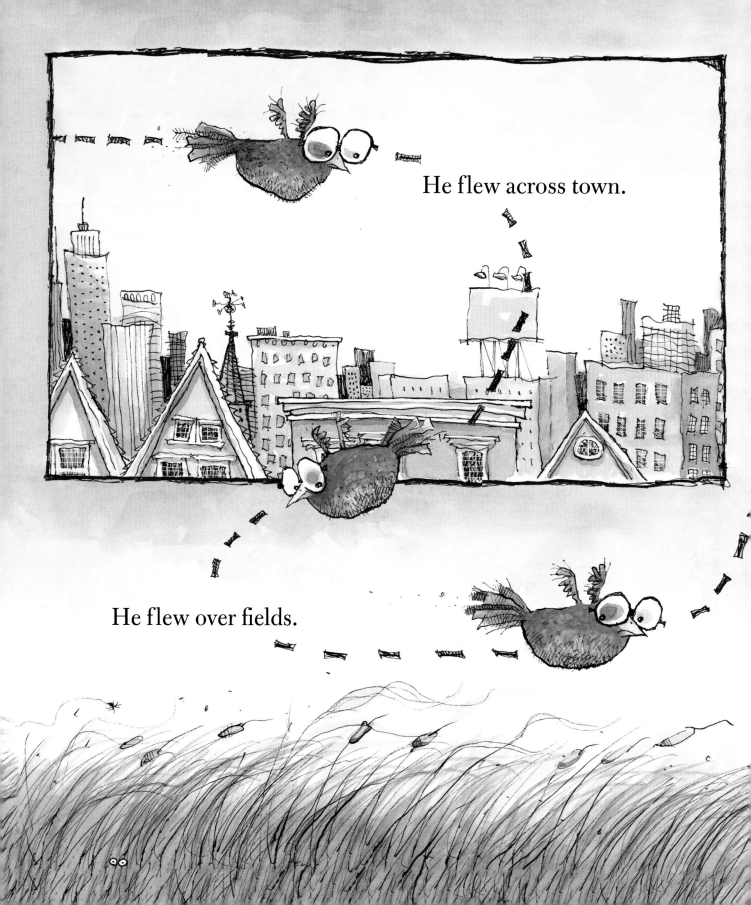

He flew across town.

He flew over fields.

Until he spotted her. Vulture blended right into the branches of the dead oak tree. But Nerdy Birdy knew his best friend a mile away.

"I WAS A BIRD BRAIN."

Vulture said nothing.

"I SHOULDN'T HAVE TWEETED THAT PHOTO OF OF YOU."

Vulture said nothing.

"I'M SORRY,"
said Nerdy Birdy.

"YOU SHOULD BE,"
said Vulture.

"I REALLY AM."

And he really was.

Nerdy Birdy shrugged.

"ONE REAL LIVE YOU IS WORTH A THOUSAND TWEETSTER FRIENDS."

This is Nerdy Birdy.

This is Vulture.

They are very different.
They are also
best friends.

Some days, Nerdy Birdy decides what they should do.

Some days,
Vulture decides
what they
should do.

And some days
they even get
together. . .

Text copyright © 2017 by Aaron Reynolds • Illustrations copyright © 2017 by Matt Davies • A Neal Porter Book • Published by Roaring Brook Press
Roaring Brook Press is a division of Holtzbrinck Publishing Holdings Limited Partnership • 175 Fifth Avenue, New York, New York 10010

The art for this book was created using pen and ink and watercolor on paper. • mackids.com •

Library of Congress Cataloging-in-Publication Data

Names: Reynolds, Aaron, 1970– author. | Davies, Matt (Matthew Keiland Parry), 1966– illustrator.

Title: Nerdy Birdy tweets / Aaron Reynolds, Matt Davies.

Description: New York : Roaring Brook Press, 2017. | Summary: Spending all of his time on social media making online friends, Nerdy Birdy neglects his
live friend, Vulture.

Identifiers: LCCN 2016038470 | ISBN 9781626721289 (hardback)

Subjects: | CYAC: Friendship—Fiction. | Social media—Fiction. | Birds—Fiction. | Vultures—Fiction. | BISAC: JUVENILE FICTION / Social Issues /
Friendship. | JUVENILE FICTION / Social Issues / Emotions & Feelings. | JUVENILE FICTION / Animals / Birds.

Classification: LCC PZ7.R33213 Nh 2017 | DDC [E]—dc23

LC record available at https://lccn.loc.gov/2016038470

Our books may be purchased for promotional, educational, or business use. Please contact your local bookseller or the Macmillan
Corporate and Premium Sales Department at (800) 221-7945 ext. 5442 or by e-mail at MacmillanSpecialMarkets@macmillan.com.

First edition 2017 • Printed in China by RR Donnelley Asia Printing Solutions Ltd., Dongguan City, Guandong Province

1 3 5 7 9 10 8 6 4 2